I am an Aro Publishing Twenty Word Book

My twenty words are:

Elmo	at
is	chickens
a	dirt
little	ducks
pig	hurt
when	rise
he	flies
gets	sighs
mad	sign
big	size

ISBN 0-89868-161-8 — Library Bound
ISBN 0-89868-162-6 — Soft Bound

FUNNY FARM BOOKS

Elmo the Pig

Story by Wendy Kanno
Pictures by Bob Reese

 ARO PUBLISHING

Elmo is

a little pig.

When he gets mad,

he gets big.

He gets mad at chickens.

He gets mad at dirt.

He gets mad at ducks.

He gets mad when hurt.

Elmo is

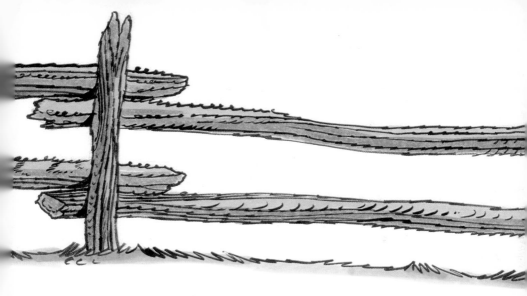

a little pig.

When he gets mad,

he gets big.

When he gets big,

he gets a rise.

When he gets big-big,

Elmo flies.

When he gets big-big,

Elmo sighs.

He is a pig sign,

Elmo size.